KU-379-921

This book belongs to

....

....

To Geoff, Sara, Tom,
Kim, Charlie and Barney

First published in Great Britain by HarperCollins Publishers Ltd in 1996.
ISBN 0 00 761364 4
Text and illustrations copyright © Andy Ellis 1996
The author asserts the moral right to be identified as the author of
this work. A CIP catalogue record for this title is available from
the British Library. All rights reserved. No part of this publication
may be reproduced, stored in a retrieval system, or transmitted in
any form or by any means, electronic, mechanical, photocopying,
recording or otherwise, without the prior permission of
HarperCollins Publishers Ltd, 77-85 Fulham Palace Road,
Hammersmith, London W6 8JB.
Printed and bound in Singapore.

The Bears' Picnic

Andy Ellis

Collins
An Imprint of HarperCollinsPublishers

It was Uncle Guzzly's birthday.

The little bears were helping with a
surprise picnic.

"Please don't make a mess," said Mum.

Billy sat on
the biscuits.

"Try not to drop any food," said Dad.

Mattie dropped
the custard.

At last they were ready to leave.
"Remember," called Mum, "you must not
eat anything until Uncle Guzzly arrives."

The little bears set off through the woods...

...and reached the picnic spot without dropping a thing. Well, almost!

"Remember," said Mattie, "we must not eat anything until Uncle Guzzly arrives."

"But no one said anything about nibbling," smiled Maude.

"Or licking," said Claude.

"Or taking a bite," laughed Billy.

Deep in their hearts they knew they were wrong, but bears can wait for only so long!

Suddenly, they heard footsteps.
"Look, it's Uncle Guzzly," cried Maude.
"Oh, what a mess we've made," gasped
Mattie.

"I think we should hide," whispered Billy.

"A picnic! What a surprise!"
cried Uncle Guzzly. "I'll
just have a nibble...

...or perhaps a lick
and a bite."

Deep in his heart he knew he was wrong,
but a bear can wait for only so long!

Suddenly, Uncle Guzzly heard footsteps.
"Oh, what a mess I've made," he said.
"I'd better find somewhere to hide."

It was Mum and Dad.

"Who has been eating our picnic?"
gasped Mum.
"And where are those naughty bears?"
asked Dad.

Down they tumbled, all in a heap,

Billy and
Maude and Mattie
and Claude.

"I told you not to eat anything until
Uncle Guzzly arrived," said Mum.
"But Mum..." cried Maude.

Suddenly from high up in the trees came
a very loud CRACK! and...

down tumbled

Uncle Guzzly!

"Surprise!" he cried.

"Oh, Uncle Guzzly!" said Mum.
"At least we've still got your birthday
cake," laughed Dad.

"Happy birthday, Uncle Guzzly!" the
bears all sang. "Now blow out the candles,
one, two, three... BLOW!"